by Michael Dahl

illustrated by Marilisa Cotroneo

Raintree is an imprint of Capstone Global Library
Limited, a company incorporated in England and
Wales having its registered office at 264 Banbury
Road, Oxford, OX2 7DY – Registered company
number: 6695582

www.raintree.co.uk
myorders@raintree.co.uk

ISBN 978 1 4747 8557 0

Designed by Tim Palin and Ashlee Suker
Production by Laura Manthe
Originated by Capstone Global Library Ltd
Printed and bound in India

Acknowledgements
Shutterstock: ALEXEY GRIGOREV, design element, vavectors, design
element, Zaie, design element

British Library Cataloguing in Publication Data
A full catalogue record for this book is available from the British
Library.

CONTENTS

CHAPTER ONE
THE EMPTY PLAYGROUND

Wind howled through the empty playground.

School was over for the day. It was dark, and Howard was alone.

Swings moved back and forth
in the wind. The chains holding the
swings clanked softly.

Howard thought it was as if
someone invisible were sitting
there.

Howard walked slowly towards the swings. He dropped his backpack on the ground.

He pulled himself onto the nearest seat and started swinging his legs.

Up and up he swung! The chains rubbed against the overhead bar that held them.

MMMMMMMMM

It was the sound zombies made in scary movies.

Finally, the swing rose so high that the chains went slack.

"I did it!" Howard whispered to himself.

Earlier that day, Howard's friend Molly had dared him.

"I bet you can't go really high on those swings," she began. "In the dark."

This will show her, thought Howard.

BOOM! CRASH!

Thunder rumbled in the dark clouds overhead.

Howard went to pick up his backpack.

His backpack was gone!

CHAPTER TWO

BEHIND HIM

Where was his backpack? Howard knew he had dropped it next to the swings.

Has someone taken it? he wondered.

He was the only person at the playground.

The swings swayed harder in the wind.

Howard looked past them. His backpack was on the other side of the playground.

How did it get there?

KA-BOOM!

More thunder boomed!

Howard wanted to get home
before it started raining. He fetched
his backpack and slipped it on.

Howard hurried down the dark path. He could see the gate to the town cemetery up ahead.

He hated walking past it, but this was the quickest way home.

Howard ran past the gate.

Suddenly he heard a strange humming sound. Then something touched his shoulder!

Howard yelled and turned around but there was no one there.

He gripped his backpack and ran.

BUZZ! BUZZ!

It sounded like a large insect
buzzing behind him.

Then something touched his arm.

"Leave me alone!" yelled Howard.

He felt a tug on his shoulders. Something inside his backpack was buzzing and moving around.

He screamed and dropped the pack on the ground!

CHAPTER THREE
WHO'S THERE?

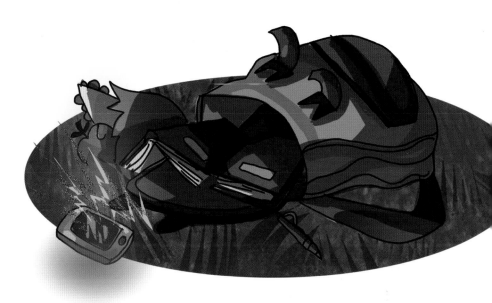

Howard's books and lunch box tumbled out of his backpack.

Then he saw it. A strange phone had fallen onto the path.

It was buzzing.

Whose phone is that? Howard wondered.

His parents had given him a phone to use but only in emergencies. The phone on the ground was not his.

BUZZ! BUZZ!!

Someone was calling him.

The boy picked up the phone
and pressed the button.

Howard gulped. "Uh, hello . . ."
he said weakly.

"*You!*" came a voice on the other
end of the phone.

Howard started to sweat.

"You!" said the voice again.

"You have my phone, and I have yours. Somehow they got swapped."

Howard let out a huge sigh
of relief. There was no ghost or
zombie following him after all.

"We should swap phones back,"
said Howard.

"Yes!" said the voice. "Can you
bring it to me?"

"Yes," said Howard. "Where do you live?"

KA-BOOM!

The thunder boomed.

"In the cemetery," said the voice. "I'm the third gravestone from the left."

AUTHOR

Michael Dahl is the author of more than 200 books for children and young adults, including graphic novels, the Library of Doom adventure series, the Dragonblood books, Trollhunters and the Hocus Pocus Hotel mystery series. Dahl has spoken at schools, libraries and conferences across the US and the UK. He currently lives in Minnesota, USA, in a haunted house.

ILLUSTRATOR

Marilisa Cotroneo lives in Rome, Italy, where she obtained a master's degree in Visual Development at IDEA Academy. As an illustrator, she uses many techniques, ranging from pencil to watercolour to digital painting. Cotroneo loves having a good laugh, drawing next to her deaf cat, Ophelia, and immersing herself in old myths and legends.

GLOSSARY

cemetery a place where dead people are buried

emergency something that needs attention straight away

fetch to go and get something

gravestone a stone marker that shows where someone is buried

groan a low moaning sound that a person or animal might make

rumble a deep, rolling sound, like thunder

slack to loosen up; not be stiff or tight

DISCUSSION QUESTIONS

1. Howard stayed out at the park late because someone had dared him to. Do you think that was a clever thing for him to do? Why or why not? Do you think he'll ever do another dare?

2. How do you think the strange phone got inside Howard's backpack?

3. What is your favourite illustration in the book? Why?

WRITING PROMPTS

1. Writing scary stories can be a lot of fun!
    Try writing your own scary story to share.

2. Howard thought something scary was
    inside his backpack. Draw a picture of
    something creepy that would fit inside
    a backpack. Write a few sentences to
    describe what it is.

3. If you picked up a strange phone, what
    spooky thing might you hear coming
    from the other end? Write down what you
    heard and share it with the class.

SCARED SILLY JOKES!

Why are cemetery gates locked?
So many people are dying to get inside!

Why didn't the ghost go to the ball?
It had no body to dance with!

Why can't you bury people who live next to a cemetery?
They're not dead yet!

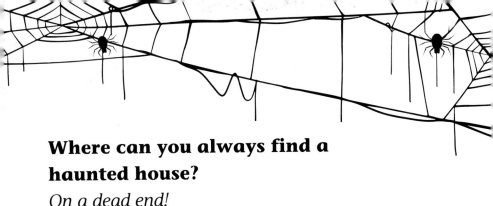

Where can you always find a haunted house?

On a dead end!

How do ghosts stay cool in the summer?

With a scare-conditioning!

What do ghosts like to eat in their sandwiches?

Scream cheese!

When do ghosts wake up?

In the moaning!

What's the first thing ghosts do when they get in a car?

Put on their sheet belts!

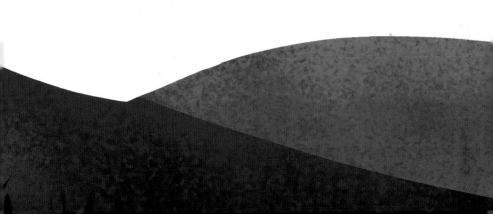

BOO BOOKS

Discover more just-right frights

Only from RAINTREE!